Gregory and Alexander

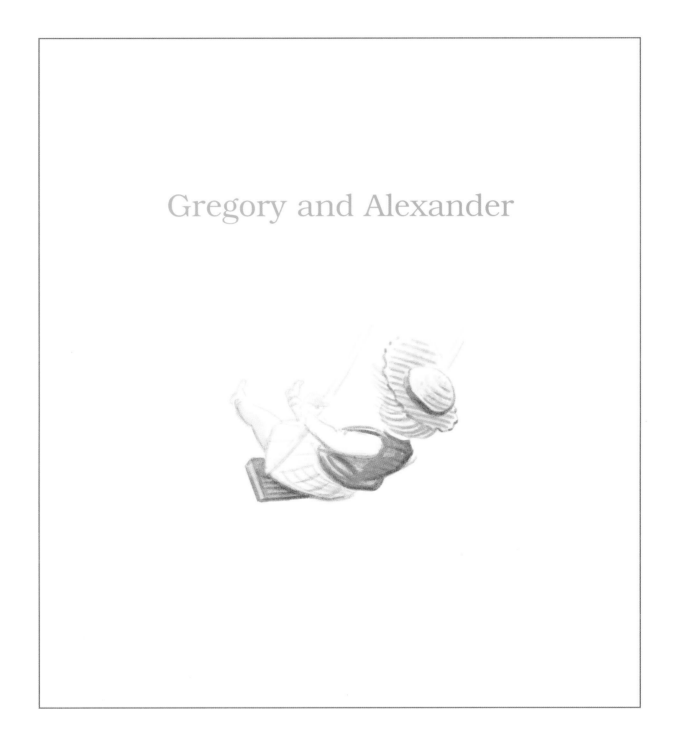

Gregory and Alexander

written by William Barringer
illustrated by Kim LaFave

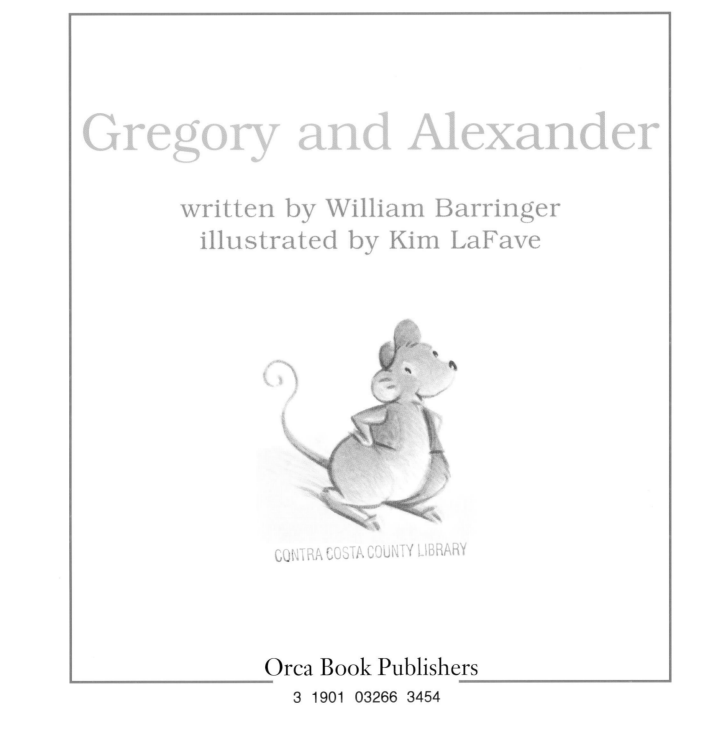

Orca Book Publishers

There once was a fine young mouse named Gregory. He lived in Perambulator Park, surviving mostly on seeds and breadcrumbs and little bits of cheese he found under the picnic tables.

Gregory made his home in a tiny hole at the bottom of an extremely large tree. His best friend, Al the caterpillar, lived nearby on the leaves of a milkweed plant.

Gregory and Al were best
friends because, once, when the
Collector Woman came into
the park and put Al the
caterpillar into a little plastic
bottle, Gregory chewed a hole
in that bottle and set Al free.

The Collector Woman was
angry. "Now where did that fat
little caterpillar go?" she
shouted.

Gregory and Al liked to watch the children playing in the park, shooting down the slides, pumping on the swings and climbing all over the monkey bars.

Sometimes at night, when everybody had gone home, Gregory would try those things himself. The mouse was very good on the slide, but could not do anything on the swings unless there was a strong wind to push him.

One summer night when the moon was full, Al the caterpillar stopped nibbling on milkweed leaves and joined Gregory in a race down the slide. It was very slippery, and both mouse and caterpillar tumbled into a heap at the bottom. Gregory rolled Al back up to the top and they tumbled down again.

A few nights later, however, Gregory huffed and puffed, but he couldn't roll Al up the slide. "You're getting fatter and fatter – too heavy for a mouse like me," he told his friend. So, Al sat happily nibbling his leaves and watched his friend play through the night.

What Gregory and Al
liked most of all was when
the children flew their kites.
What kites they were!
Tiger kites.
Eagle kites.
Airplane kites.
Box kites.
Japanese fighting kites.

The children raced
around. Their kites climbed
and swooped and did loop-
the-loops and floated in the
sky like angels.
Of course, sometimes
they crashed or got stuck in
the trees, too.

"I would love to fly a kite," said Gregory to himself, "but they are all so big. They would pull me off the ground and I might never come down."

That night he snuck downtown to a toy store. Many wonderful kites were displayed in the window, but not one kite was small enough for a mouse.

"Rats," muttered Gregory.

The next morning, Gregory's whiskers dragged in the dust. "What's the matter with you?" said Al the caterpillar.

"I can't find a single kite my own size," Gregory grumbled.

"Is that all?" said Al. "I will get you a kite – but you will have to wait."

"How long?" asked Gregory, who was not a patient mouse.

"Just you wait," said Al.

After nibbling through a last leaf, he climbed into the branches of Gregory's tree, where he tucked himself up in a little blanket and proceeded to take a nap.

"Phooey," said the mouse.

So Gregory waited.
And waited.
And waited some more. But the caterpillar did not come back.

Gregory tried racing on the slide alone. He even played with a friendly spider, but nothing felt quite right.

One night the mouse climbed the tree. But he could not find the branch with the blanket. He looked and looked, but all he found was a wisp of the blanket snagged on a twig.

He called Al's name. It echoed in the quiet night. There was no answer.

"I miss him," thought Gregory. "I hope the Collector Woman didn't catch him again."

The days got shorter and the nights got cooler.

One morning a beautiful orange-and-black butterfly fluttered down from the top of the tree.

"Hello, Gregory," he said.

"Do I know you?" asked the mouse.

"In a way," said the butterfly. "I used to be Al the caterpillar, but now I am Alexander the butterfly. I slept and dreamed inside my chrysalis, and while I was sleeping I was transformed."

"My goodness!" squeaked Gregory.

"What's more," said Alexander, "I am a Monarch – the king of butterflies."

"A king," said the mouse softly.

"And now, my friend," said Alexander, "I am going to turn into something else again – your kite!"

And so he did. With the help of the friendly spider, they attached a long silky line to Alexander's middle and the other end to a small stick. Gregory held the stick and scurried across Perambulator Park at full speed.

Alexander soared.

Alexander swooped.

Alexander dived.

Alexander looped the loop.

Alexander was the best kite in the park – he never crashed or got stuck in the trees – and Gregory was the happiest mouse.

They played for days and days as the leaves turned from green to gold and red and began to fall to the ground. One dark day the Collector Woman came back to the park.

"Aha!" she cried. "I've been hunting for you and now I've got you."

She scooped up Alexander into her big round net.

Gregory was shocked – and frightened – and then extremely angry. He jumped upon the Collector Woman's worn-out running shoe and nibbled furiously at her big toe.

"Ouch!" screamed the Collector Woman. "A mad mouse! A vicious mouse! Mouse attack! Mouse attack!"

She dropped her net and ran hollering out of the park. Alexander floated to freedom.

"You are a brave mouse and a true friend," Alexander told Gregory. "You have saved me twice. But I must save my own life this time. I must leave you now."

"But why?" said Gregory, so sadly.

"The warm days are ending. The cold dark days are coming, and I would freeze if I stayed here," said the butterfly. "I am going to fly south where it is always sunny."

"Will I ever see you again?" asked Gregory.

"No," said Alexander. "But I think that next summer you will meet another caterpillar. I hope that you teach him to tumble and roll on the slide. Perhaps he will become your new kite. Goodbye, my friend."

Gregory watched until Alexander was a tiny orange dot in the deep blue sky and then was gone forever.

Now, if you should go to Perambulator Park to fly your kite next summer, you might just see an orange-and-black butterfly doing a loop-the-loop near an extremely large tree.

And if you look very closely, down below the Monarch, you might just see a fine young mouse dashing through the grass.

If you do, be sure to leave Gregory some breadcrumbs or a bit of cheese under the picnic table.

National Library of Canada Cataloguing in Publication Data

Barringer, William.

Gregory and Alexander / William Barringer ; [illustrations by] Kim LaFave.

ISBN 1-55143-252-8

I. LaFave, Kim. II. Title.

PS8553.A771638G73 2003   jC813'.6   C2002-911155-2

PZ7.B2754Gr 2003

First published in the United States, 2003

Library of Congress Control Number: 2002112908

Summary: Gregory the mouse and Al the caterpillar are best friends until Al wraps himself up in a blanket and goes to sleep high in a tree.

Teachers' Guide available from Orca Book Publishers.

Orca Book Publishers gratefully acknowledges the support for its publishing programs provided by the following agencies: the Government of Canada through the Department of Canadian Heritage, the Canada Council for the Arts, and the British Columbia Arts Council.

Design: Christine Toller
Printed and bound in Hong Kong

IN CANADA:
Orca Book Publishers
1030 North Park Street
Victoria, BC Canada
V8T 1C6

IN THE UNITED STATES:
Orca Book Publishers
PO Box 468
Custer, WA   USA
98240-0468

05 04 03 • 5 4 3 2 1